DREAM OR REALITY

FICTIONAL STORY

KHYATI SRIVASTAVA

Contents

PREFACE

<u>DREAM OR REALITY?</u>

This title is a question in itself, isn't the story dream of someone or an actual incident had happened in this story? but actually not! It will definitely be going to make you read this story as well as share it with others.

The beginning begins with the main character of this story listening to a bedtime story from her Grandpa!

that story only turns into something such as this could not be imaginable.

For further details, Go and read the book !

I

Emily's Morning

It was a long time ago,
In a beautiful and amidst dense valleys, behind a beautiful and vast spring of flowing water there was a hidden door, which goes to a golden kingdom straight a way . What happened next, tell me grandfather? ... Emily asked excitedly."No it's time for you to reach to your bed,now" Grandpa replied. Emily went to her bed immediately but her mind was constantly on wondering about what had happened next to the story. Suddenly one querry poped in her mind that was it a fictional story or a real one? She thought to ask her grandpa but it was too late in night. Impetuously, a fluttering thin shiny gold leaf entered into the room. Emily was about to go
to her bed when she caught her sight of that Golden and Shiny Leaf. As she went near it ... .

II

Teleportation

A big Flash of light bright as Sun. That bright light left Emily in a dark cave. As she opened her eyes, she was shocked, she could not understand how she reached this deserted cave from her comfortable room. She tried to find her way, moving forward she saw a light coming from some distance. While following that light, she had reached the other end of the cave, but then she heard her mother's voice. Her mother was very worried and was looking for her, Emily thought why not to go back and will come back after returning from school.She goes back to retun home but was still worried that how will she return and from where? Will she be able to go or not? thinking all this she was going in reverse direction when she saw a door which was just behind the cupboard of her room

III

Golden Kingdom

She goes to school but the incident of the night kept her mind distracted, she was just in a hurry that when she reached home and when she could know the secret of that golden leaf, what could be on the other side of that cave, and the biggest question it was, Why and how did all this happen to me? as soon as she reached home, she neither ate food not talked to anyone, she immediately went to that cave, moving slowly when she came to the other end, her eyes were closed from the outside light. After trying a little, when she was able to open her eyes, a kingdom made of gold spread over a vast area in front of her.

Seeing all this, her condition worsened, she cannot believe that whatever she is seeing, is it true. Before she could understand anything, a huge dragon appeared in front of her. He gestured to Emily to sit on him, she thought it best to obey him. That dragon takes him on a tour of the open sky, while making him enjoy the cool breeze, makes him land in the middle of the palace of that kingdom. As soon as Emily gets down, some soldiers come to welcome her, sit in a big palanquin and take her inside the palace.Everything inside that grand palace was so beautiful, it was all like a dream, but Emily had to believe it all. As soon as Emily enters the assembly, she is greeted with thunderous applause and showers of flowers. Emily was shocked to see all this and just now her patience broke, she screamed and asked, "What is all this happening? Is it all for me, if yes! Then why?". Eerie silence prevailed in the whole assembly.A beautiful queen was sitting on a big throne in front, but the real throne which was in the middle was empty. After I screamed, a minister sitting there got up and said, "Victory to the Queen! You are welcome, Queen! We are grateful to have seen you after thousands of years." Emily was shocked again. "Did you call me queen?", Emily asks in bewilderment."Yes!", replied the minister. "I don't understand what all this is eating you.", Emily said. Then the queen stands up and asks a maid to take Emily to the guest room. she goes with them. On the way, she asks the maid, "Whatever was said in that meeting, is it all true?" "Yes!", answered the maid. "Here is your room, Queen!" The maid leaves, Emily is deeply worried, until the queen of the assembly comes into Emily's room and says, "I know you must be very upset, just now you have come here and come You have been told so many unknown things and especially so many big things, but don't worry, I am with you.Now you sit here comfortably and I will tell you what happened and who are you?"

Thousands of years ago, everyone lived happily in the kingdom of our brilliant and great queen Jaintia. One day our State Counsellor died, our Queen announced a competition to elect a new State Counsellor. There was a common minister named Chivaku in our cabinet. He was a very cunning type of person, there was no limit to his desires. He used a very cheap trick to get the post of state advisor. He fed such a fruit full of intoxication to all the candidates, from which no one could get up for two days, at the same time he killed everyone as soon as they fainted and fed that fruit to our queen as soon as she *fainted, he gave her a The intelligence was leading to the spot but our queen had pretended to be unconscious, she only wanted to find out the real culprit. Knowing all this, she tried to run away by jumping from his vehicle, but that Chivaku pushes her from a big waterfall and after that day he reigns for some days that suddenly one day, in the sky Clouds come and the weather turns bad, then there is a voice from the sky that," What do you think Chivaku, to destroy your sinful kingdom soon, thousand years from now a girl named "Emily" will come to destroy you, she It is none other than Queen Jaintia!!!!! Your doom is certain Chivaku! It is certain!" On hearing all this, Chivaku disappeared from where, people say that he is collecting some magical powers to escape from you.*

IV
Reamrkable War

There is a very loud sound of devastation, everyone's screams come from outside. The Queen stands up and tells Emily, "It's time, Queen Emily, to put an end to this tyrant!" "But, but how can I? What can I do?", Emily asks fearfully. "You have absolutely no need to be afraid, Your Highness!!" The Queen takes the crown off her head, and puts it on Emily. Magic works. Emily's clothes change into a royal outfit and she gets magical powers as well as her faithful pet dragon approaches her and Emily climbs on top of him. "You can! Your Highness! Destroy him and save us.

A different confidence had come inside Emily, she felt that yes this is my kingdom and I have to save it.
In front, the demon Chivaku, equipped with infinite powers, was doing his atrocities.
As soon as Emily put her hand towards him, it was as if some divine power helped her and such a powerful energy comes out inside her that it hurts her too much when it comes out. That tyrannical, cunning, hypocrite came to an end but Emily also fell from the top of the dragon and was badly injured. When she opened her eyes after some time,

she was surprised because she was lying on the bed of her room. Surprisingly, Emily moves her cupboard and sees that Golden and Shiny Leaf, Seeing which Emily's face blossoms like a rose, she starts moving round and round with joy, when her mother's voice sounds, "Emily, it's time to eat, come quickly, and yes! Come after washing your hands." "Yes mother!"

GrandPa calls,"Emily your story is left unfinished"

SOMETHING LEFT!!!

The story is left just wait for the next part to be published

• 9 •

Secret Letter

A secret letter came to Emily from behind the cupboard.

Marvellous Decision

Emily decidd to go back to the kingdom ONCE AGAIN!!